NOTHING IN BETWEEN ONE

SCARLETT FINN

Also by Scarlett Finn

GO NOVELS
GO WITH IT
GO IT ALONE
GO ALL OUT
GO ALL IN
GO FULL CIRCLE

EXILE
HIDE & SEEK
KISS CHASE

WRECK & RUIN
RUIN ME
RUIN HIM

**THE BRANDED
SERIES**
BRANDED
SCARRED
MARKED

**FORBIDDEN
PREQUEL DUET**
ALL. ONLY.
ONLY YOURS

THE FORBIDDEN NOVELS
FORBIDDEN DESIRE
FORBIDDEN WANT
FORBIDDEN WISH
FORBIDDEN NEED
FORBIDDEN BOND

**BOMBSHELLS & BILLIONAIRES
(ROXIVERSE)**
NOTHING TO HIDE
NOTHING TO LOSE
NOTHING IN BETWEEN: ONE
NOTHING TO DECLARE
NOTHING TO US
NOTHING IN BETWEEN: TWO
NOTHING TO SAY
NOTHING TO GAIN
NOTHING IN BETWEEN: THREE
NOTHING TO YOU
NOTHING TO THIS PREQUEL: ONE WILD NIGHT
NOTHING TO THIS
NOTHING IN BETWEEN: FOUR
NOTHING TO DO
NOTHING TO NO ONE
NOTHING TO FEAR
NOTHING TO DENY
NOTHING TO BEAT
NOTHING TO THE WEDDING
NOTHING TO TELL
NOTHING TO IT
NOTHING TO SEE
NOTHING TO WIN
NOTHING TO OFFER
NOTHING TO PROVE

**LOVE AGAINST THE ODDS
STANDALONE COLLECTION**
SWEET SEAS
HEIR'S AFFAIR
RESCUED
MAESTRO'S MUSE
GETTING TRICKY
THIRTEEN
REMEMBER WHEN...
RELUCTANT SUSPICION
XY FACTOR

KINDRED SERIES
RAVEN
SWALLOW
CUCKOO
SWIFT
FALCON
FINCH

MISTAKE DUET
MISTAKE ME NOT
SLEIGHT MISTAKE

LOST & FOUND
LOST
FOUND

**THE EXPLICIT
SERIES**
EXPLICIT INSTRUCTION
EXPLICIT DETAIL
EXPLICIT MEMORY

TO DIE FOR...
TO DIE FOR TRUTH
TO DIE FOR HONOR
TO DIE FOR VIRTUE
TO DIE FOR DUTY
TO DIE FOR LOVE

**RISQUÉ & HARROW
INTERTWINED**
TAKE A RISK
FIGHTING FATE
RISK IT ALL
FIGHTING BACK
GAME OF RISK

ONE

REALITY HAD NEVER been so dreamlike. Going through the motions of the show, smiling and laughing, playing the part, it was odd to think she'd never really done the chat show interview thing before. Maybe being next to Zairn bolstered her confidence. Next to the man she loved. The man she'd announced her love for without knowing if he wanted her back. What a stupid thought, of course he wanted her back. He'd known they were forever long before stupid her figured it out.

Confidence wasn't exactly a problem for her pre-big-announcement-to-the-universe. Still, knowing Zairn would support her no matter what gave a whole new meaning to the word. This was her life now. With him. Beside him. They were a team. Equals. He'd given her the world. Literally. It would take a lifetime to show him how much she wished to do the same.

"And we're out," a Headset Guy called.

Everyone started moving and talking. The crew. The audience. Talk at Sunset was over for another night. It was time to clear out. Those required to stay silent and still were now free. All were free. Including her.

Pinned to her man's side, Roxanna Kyst was happy

to stay on the couch and let activity flourish everywhere else. The audience prepared to leave, putting on jackets and checking purses. The crew did their duties, probably eager to get home. Everyone had purpose. Hers was to stay right there. At her guy's side.

Talk at Sunset host, Drew Harvey, shifted to the edge of his seat. "Drinks on you tonight, Z?"

"Yeah," the musician from the other end of the couch spoke up. "You got the girl, I say drinks are on you."

"Not my decision," Zairn said, squeezing her knee.

All focus landed on her.

"What do you say, Future Mrs. Lomond?" Drew Harvey asked. "Want to invite us to your party?"

Sounded like a damper on the night she'd envisioned. "Oh, uh, sure," she said, figuring they should be thankful to those who'd facilitated their reunion. "I have to go back to the hotel to change first."

"You look great!"

"Yeah, I know," she said, flashing the men a smile. "I like to look extra great for Crimson."

Zairn stood, taking her hand to draw her to her feet. "We'll meet you there."

Drew Harvey laughed. "If you get your girl back to the hotel, I don't think we'll see you 'til the next time you're in town."

Zairn scooped a protective arm around her. "That's the hope,"

The others stood. "We'll start a pool. See if anyone gets close to how long it takes you to show."

"Do that."

As Zairn was about to step past, the host grabbed his arm. "You will call ahead about the free drinks though, right?"

Zairn laughed. "Don't think I've seen you pay for a drink in your life, Drew. Think they stopped counting your tab when it hit five figures."

Jovial laughter followed them to the curtain at the back of the set. In the rear corridor, people hurried around, moving things, talking to this person and that. Bustle charged the air. Though the guy holding her hand didn't seem to notice.

Ignoring everyone and everything, Zairn led her through the organized chaos and outside to a familiar alley. The one Astrid used when they first exited the building after Roxie's win.

Just like then, a driver stood next to an open rear car door, waiting for them. Once they were inside, the door closed.

"How do they do that?" she asked. "Know when you're leaving, or do they just stand there all night? What if it's raining?"

"I don't know," Zairn said, his fingertips gliding up her thigh. "I guess they get wet."

The moment the car started moving, his lips met hers. Though they hadn't been parted for long, it felt like a lifetime since they'd last had privacy. Silence. Passion. Could it really be happening? Were they really there? Together. Alone. His hand on her skin, the insistence of his lips…

With any other guy in the past, she'd be terrified of the certainty. But it wasn't frightening or upsetting, it was enlivening, invigorating. No part of her held doubt. His lips were so sure, determined, yet they spoiled hers like they were forging new territory, learning each other all over again.

Love. Real love. Like theirs, it was more valuable than any gold or jewels, and definitely rarer. Being together was their duty, she couldn't flout their connection, their chemistry, their magnetism.

And they'd almost lost it.

Lost each other.

Because of her.

So much had happened in such a short time that some details were still hazy. Not all details. The most important thing, their love, was crystal clear.

Stroking his chest, she pressured him away just enough to murmur, "We should talk."

"Mm hmm," he said, kissing her again.

It wasn't difficult to surrender. Her lips wouldn't behave, they sought his, eager to be joined in delight… and devouring desire. He'd come back for her. They were together. The right way. Completely. Having him again was a thrill… With Zairn, everything was a thrill.

The persistence of her hands became aggressive until she was pulling at him. Their closeness wasn't enough. They shouldn't give into the physical, not before they talked it out. Did he know forever meant forever? Had she made herself clear?

The delicate glide of his deft fingertips on her inner thigh tempted her legs to open wider. He wanted access and it wasn't in her to deny him.

In their eleven days, car journeys often meant clandestine opportunities to slake their desire. Their first hours together—together, together—were proving to be just as satisfying.

"I have questions and I have to—"

He kissed her hard. "It's been weeks, Lola," he breathed against her, stroking her through her panties. "Don't ask me to wait when I need you, baby."

Damn, she'd missed him. Missed them. "How much do you want me?" she teased, leaning back to keep her mouth just out of reach of his. "You need me bad?"

The drowsy fog in his aroused gaze teased her right back. "I'll always be chasing you."

Curling her fingers into his shirt, she pulled herself against him. "You caught me, Casanova. Promise you'll never let me go."

Their wild hormones took precedence over everything else. He was right. They needed each other. Having come so close to losing them, they both needed the reassurance. They needed to seal their reunion, to prove it was no dream. That moment, that union was needed to show their love was real, solid, and that it wouldn't be taken away.

Their kiss in the studio, on international television, was nothing to the depth of his kiss in the back of that private car. Soon, hands found zippers, she climbed onto his lap, and slid down onto him.

Bliss. He was her bliss. Her love. Her future.

Rising and falling, the momentum of their love deepened her need to please him… and please herself. This man would be the last one ever inside her, she'd be his last too. Acknowledging those truths should put their lives in perspective, yet it felt too big, too much for one person to shoulder alone.

"Z," she whispered, moving on him. Grabbing his head, she took his mouth from her chest to join their eyes. "I love you."

His lazy smile spurred her to work harder. "I know."

Everything in the universe clicked into place. Realizing her love was one thing, her mission to get him back had given her purpose. What would happen after hadn't crossed her mind. Him showing up on Talk at Sunset wasn't even in the ballpark of her wildest imaginings. Expressing the truth of her love was her goal. Showing him that not only did she want him, but that she was proud of them, meant everything in that moment.

"Say it to me," she said, distracted by his hands sliding from her breasts to her hips. "I want you to say it to me. Please."

"Love you," he said with an almost snicker behind the words. "Is this real or did I fall and hit my head?"

"Does it matter?" she asked, guiding his fingertips to her lips. "So long as we're together, I don't care where we are."

"You finally got it."

"Better late than never," she said as his arms came around her. "Thank you for coming back."

"Thank you for being you," he said, wrapping his arms around her to guide her onto her back on the seat.

"I'm sorry I was so… thick."

His lips brushed her hairline. The subtle sign was acceptance enough. "I've missed being inside you."

And she'd missed having him there. Nothing would keep them apart again. Embracing the truth she'd been hiding from herself was liberating. He'd known. He had to. Why else would he come back? Yeah, they needed to talk, but words would come after action.

TWO

"WE'RE TERRIBLE HOSTS," Roxie said, her hands falling to her damp chest.

"They'll get over it. The drinks are free. They won't notice we're not there."

Their hotel bedroom was too dark for her to read the wall clock. When they got there, the drapes were already closed… weren't they? She'd been more interested in the man stripping her than the soft furnishings.

His phone had been going nuts. In the car. On the way up to the room. Probably during their tryst too, but her mind had been elsewhere then. He hadn't checked it until just a moment ago. Within their congratulatory messages, more than a few people mentioned celebrating at the club. Something her guy was definitely used to hearing. Various people, famous and not, wanted to shake their hands and kiss their cheeks. He sent out a blanket reply, inviting everyone to the VIP area in Crimson LA. Only, oopsy, the couple wouldn't make it to the party.

Talk at Sunset aired at midnight. Sex in the car. Sex in the hotel. It would probably be too late to get into the club. A lot of those people could be turned away. Celebrity or not.

She laughed and rolled toward him. "You own the building. We'd get in after hours, right?"

"Whatever you want, Lola."

"I want you," she said, propping her chin on his pec. "I love you."

"Which I found out on national television."

"International television," she said as his fingers opened to capture her hair. "You knew it, didn't you? That I loved you. Before even I did."

"I knew it in the bathroom," he said, bobbing his chin in that general direction. "When you asked me to hold you."

"When you walked away…" she teased, pushing her chin into him. "After dumping me."

"On the Triple Seven, the grief in your voice… That was it. Reality hit. What I thought was reality. Fun was what you wanted. I was too far gone to keep that going. I had to get out… loving you like I do with you just out of reach… it was torture, baby."

"One you'll never have to endure again," she said, pushing up to kiss him. "If you knew it when I was a mess in the bathroom, why did you walk away?"

He smiled. "You still had to figure it out. I was your crutch. While I was around, you didn't have to figure it out because we had each other."

"If you love something, set it free…"

"Right. And you're a determined woman. If you figured it out, you'd find some way to put us back together."

"Yeah," she said, prodding him. "But you changed your number."

"I didn't change my number. I blocked yours,"

he said. Her mouth fell open. "I made everyone block and erase your number. I had no faith in my willpower to resist needing you… I had to remove all temptation."

"But you left Knox here."

"Knox has been working in LA for a few weeks." The tilt of his lips complemented his next confession. "But I might have left instructions to accommodate your every whim, should you go to him. I've got to admit, Talk at Sunset was bold, even for you."

"I had nothing to hide," she teased. "And nothing left to lose. Besides, you broke the seal on hiding us from the press."

"I'm sorry," he said, growing more somber. "We always said what we were didn't belong to them. I shouldn't have—"

"It's okay," she said, brushing her lips across his. "That was before I got it. Now that I've got it, I get it. You were proud of us. And the world knows, so we can tell them whatever we want. They know we're together, why shouldn't we slip our love into conversation?"

His arms came around her and he flipped her onto her back, teasing her mouth with his. "My philosophy exactly."

"Say it again. Say it here in the dark. In our sex sheets."

He snickered. "I love you."

She shivered and threw her arms around his neck. "I love you too."

"And that's how this is supposed to go," he said and kissed her.

Life was going to be different with Zairn Lomond. Already it was better. Accepting her feelings was freeing. She was his and he was hers. Just as it was supposed to be.

"Do we need to talk about stuff?" she asked.

"What kind of stuff?"

"On the show, what I said about where we'll live and…" Her words trailed off to a smile that became a laugh. "This is so crazy."

"The love part or that you're finally accepting this was always where we were headed."

Her fingers combed through his hair. "You're a lot, Z… A lot. A lot." He frowned, so she traced her fingertips across his forehead. "In an amazing way. I didn't see it because, I guess, I was scared. Now that I'm over that… I can't see my future without you. Watching that footage, the way you held me, how I felt in your arms… this has to be forever, Casanova."

"Of course it's forever," he said and kissed her. "Where do you want to get married? Here? New York? London? Rome?"

"Do you care?"

His amused smile said it all. "Only about you being happy."

"I don't want to sell the rights to it, I know that for sure." Tracing his features, her heart was in awe of his dedication and its own certainty. "What do you think about a wedding planner?"

"Isn't that what the bride is for?" The sincerity of his tease earned his shoulder a fist nudge. He just laughed. "Baby, you can have whatever you want. You want doves and ice sculptures and celebrity guests, you've got it. Money is no object."

"I don't want any of that," she said as he slithered down to nuzzle her neck.

Breathing her in, he got so close that the sensation of his exhale aroused her. "So why do we need a wedding planner?"

"Because it will mean the world to her." His mouth stopped and he rose to meet her eye. "Jane. We'll ask Jane to do it. If you talk to her boss, I'm sure he'll give her time off… Especially after creepy London Guy, you know? She needs this. Planning Zairn Lomond's wedding will mean everything to her."

"What about Roxanna Kyst's wedding?"

She sighed. "Look at it this way, if it was up to me, we'd just go to Vegas and get it done."

"Fine by me." Sitting up, he caught her arm to tug on her. "Come on."

Remaining limp, she was too ensconced in their cozy den to want to move. "But not by Jane. She's a romantic. If we just blow off the wedding, it will hurt her feelings."

He let her go and considered her for a few seconds before speaking. "You want the big spectacle wedding for the sake of your friend?"

She shrugged. "Maybe."

His smile crept up slowly. "Tough girl, Roxie Kyst—"

"Hey, I never said I was a tough anything," she said, grabbing his arm to pull him back down on his side next to her. "Romantic doesn't have to mean big. She'll understand we don't want insanity and we will get final say. Intimate. That's what I want. Something intimate. Just us and the people we care about."

"Okay," he said, pushing the covers from her body. "Are you going to invite Clement?"

"I don't know. Are you going to invite Kesley?"

His gaze jumped to hers. "Now! Finally! She gives me shit for trailing an ex around."

Roxie shook her head. "Sorry to disappoint, that's not what this is. I don't mind if she's there. Her or Porter. I told you before we broke up. I understand why you need to support her and I'm secure in how you feel about me." Although at the time in Buenos Aires, love hadn't occurred to her. "Given what you do, where you spend your time, there are always going to be other women offering themselves to you. Younger, maybe even hotter women."

"Hotter than my Lola Bunny?" he asked, circling her nipple with a fingertip. "Not possible."

"Thank you," she said like she utterly believed it. "You're not going to fall out of love with me. After what it took to get us here, what you went through to get me, you're not going to jeopardize us."

"What about you?" he asked, relaxing his palm over her breast. "You'll be in demand. More so after the documentary airs. Guys will be lining up to make the conquest."

"Yeah, right," she said, her glib dismissal startled him, at least until she smiled. "I lost you already. In Crimson when you…" The ease of their mood shifted. Her intention hadn't been to darken the atmosphere but recalling that time chilled her. "I didn't want to live. Couldn't remember how to breathe."

His hand slipped across to squeeze her arm. "When I realized you were missing…"

"You thought about Dayah. I'm sorry, baby."

"Maybe I thought about her, I don't know," he said, shaking his head slightly. "But you were… I thought you didn't love me. I thought we were through with each other, but not knowing where you were…" When he blinked, his eyes opened to land on hers. "I ceased to exist. Nothing made sense. Without you, I couldn't… Shit, Lola, all I could think about was finding you and when we saw you leaving with him…"

"Nothing happened," she said without breaking eye contact while fumbling to link their hands. "He was the guy who got us arrested that first night in Crimson LA. At least, he was the guy who blocked us from getting in. We saw him when we arrived and he apologized. Thought I was going to snitch and get him fired. I asked for him to cover security for me and my girls to reassure him it wasn't like that. I know what it is to need a job."

"Unlike us billionaires," he said with a brow arch.

"He was the first person I saw when I left you in the club, I didn't know anyone else and couldn't go back to the hotel. I didn't mean to fall asleep, I was just numb."

"You say nothing happened, I believe you," he said, watching their fingers play together on her abdomen. "Let's just agree not to disappear on each other again."

"Okay," she said, freeing her fingers to push him onto his back. "Maybe we can get you chipped or something."

"I'll call Zane in the morning," he said, supporting her waist when she straddled him.

"Mr. Dyce," she said. "Does it make you feel powerful to know all these resourceful people?"

He yanked her down, wrapping both strong arms around her, clamping her against him. "This makes me feel powerful."

"Who has the reins here, Casanova," she whispered, deliberately keeping her lips just above his.

"The future Mrs. Lomond."

Damn, he knew how to turn her on. "Say it again."

A breath of laughter left his lips. "I love you."

"I love you too."

Sinking into the kiss submerged her in their security. Zairn belonged to her, and she was his. They didn't have to figure everything out overnight. So long as they leaned on each other, everything would work out in the end.

THREE

DRAGGING HER FEET, Roxie pushed her hair from her face as she left the bedroom. The sleeve of Zairn's shirt, that she'd thrown on, thwarted her effort.

Zairn's people could be around. Wandering into the living room naked wouldn't go over well, otherwise she wouldn't have bothered with the shirt.

As it turned out, his people were around. Except they were stuck in the TV. Zairn was on the opposite couch, his back to her.

"…productivity is the concern. Cost comes later."

She propped her butt on the low back of the couch and leaned back to muss Zairn's neat hair.

He caught her hand to guide it to his throat.

"Little Rox," Ballard said on the TV. "Was wondering when you'd show up."

"I missed you too," she said, twisting around to check out the screen. "You're all so tiny on there." She didn't recognize the room in the background and should because she'd stayed in other Grand LA rooms. "Where are you?"

"Rome," Ballard said.

She frowned. "That doesn't look like our Rome suite."

"Because we don't stay in top lodgings."

"Right," she said, grinning. "Because you're minions."

Zairn flashed her a smile. "You'll get used to it."

"Why didn't you bring your people with you?"

"Do we need them?" he asked. "The point was always to join them when you were ready. The Retrospective has seen enough hiccups."

"Not doing too good at this ambassador thing, am I?"

Without giving her time to ponder, he eased her closer, using his grip on her hand to pull her down. "You're perfect at it, Lola," he said, stealing her mouth with his.

"This is highly unprofessional."

They broke their kiss.

"Hi, Ogilvie," Roxie said, still gazing into Zairn. "Finally screwing an employee, baby? And you said you never would."

Zairn enjoyed her teasing.

Ogilvie? Not so much. "We're in the middle of a meeting."

"I didn't know that, I just woke up," she said, sitting straight again, her back still to the TV. "Would you rather I wait for permission to speak or knock before I walk in?"

That second one would be tough given there was no door to knock on.

"Roxie is part of the business," Zairn said, giving Ogilvie no time to reply. "I expect her to know more than any of you. She'll get my raw, kneejerk thoughts most of the time. Don't be surprised if she's the first person I consult or if I want to run something by her before making a final decision."

"You can't allow a woman to—"

"Understand?" Roxie asked. "I can listen and think at the same time. I'm not that inept. I promise I won't beg him to cash out to keep me in fur coats. I don't need his money. You keep his money. So long as I get some cock and a little sass from time to time, I'll be happy."

"You're a low maintenance woman," Zairn said, hooking an arm up over her lap. "You want to come join the meeting?"

"Have you told Ogilvie we're getting married?" she asked, peeking down at her guy.

His smirk both appreciated her honesty and betrayed he knew the temptation to play with their elder was too overpowering to resist.

"There's still time to talk him out of it," deadpan Ogilvie said with conviction.

"No time to talk him out of it," she said. Tossing a leg over the couch to straddle the back, she caressed Zairn's torso with her pointed toes. "We'll be in Vegas in a few short hours."

"Vegas?" Ogilvie bellowed.

"Before the press find out about the baby."

Her innocence wasn't so easy to maintain when Zairn's amusement grew.

Ogilvie couldn't see that and started his blustering again. "Oh for—"

"She's kidding," Zairn said, scooping a hand around her calf to direct her knee to his mouth. "There's no baby… yet."

Her lover wasn't as anti-mischief as the professional exterior wanted to portray.

Dropping forward, she wrapped an arm around his head, sinking her face into his hair. "Would you put a baby in me, baby?"

"Anytime you want," he said, stroking her leg.

"Babies? Have you called Dunlap?" Ogilvie asked. "You want the ink dry before you do anything permanent."

"Ink dry?" she asked, running her fingers through Zairn's hair, squashing her breasts against him. "On the marriage certificate?"

"You won't get near the aisle before the prenup."

"Of course! Thank you for looking out for me, Og. You're so right. He needs to know my shoes are my shoes, no matter how many years we're married."

"You've figured me out, Lo. Just give me the ring back now."

She sat up to admire it. After a moment of faux

pondering, she sighed. "Nope. Take the shoes, I want the ruby."

He wrapped his hands around her foot to kiss her instep. "You look better without them anyway."

Laying on the back of the couch, she tucked the shirt over her thighs. "Don't look better without my Empress Ruby."

"No, you do not."

Despite not taking her focus from the ring on her hand, she loved the pride in his happy voice.

It wasn't about the jewel or the price tag, the ring reminded her of them, of their happiness, their future, and how close they'd come to losing it… because of her.

"I'll call Dunlap today, get him working on it," Ogilvie said, carrying on regardless. "We'll need specifics, to cover every eventuality."

"No," Zairn said, running his fingertips down the back of her thigh to straighten her leg in front of his face, grazing it with his stubble, reminding her of the first morning they'd woken together.

"No, what?" Ogilvie asked. "You don't want Dunlap to head it up? He'll have someone who—no, you're right, we need a specialist."

"No prenup," Zairn said. "Rox and I are too go with the flow for paperwork."

Taking her leg from his grasp, she sat up. "We're having a prenup."

He shook his head like he had the final word. "No."

"You can't say no," she said. "I want a prenup."

"To say what?"

"That you're obliged to support our children, but I don't want a cent. No alimony, no fifty percent."

"Everyone heard that," Ogilvie said.

As her fingers moved into Zairn's hair again, he turned to look up at her, no humor in sight. "You won't marry me without it?"

Was this going to be another fight? Another wedge between them?

Bowing, she laid her hands on his cheeks to kiss him.

Just a quick, short one, but incredible all the same. "Getting rid of me won't be that easy," she said and kissed him again. When she pulled away, his smile was back. "But..." she prodded his shoulder, "the same is true if we sign one. I'll love you and marry you either way. Don't take that chivalrous stance you always think is necessary."

"Good," Ogilvie said. "Who did Kintyre's prenup?"

"No prenup," Zairn said, stern while he adored her. "Goddamn you're beautiful."

"Don't rule out me teaching you a lesson," she murmured, kissing him left then right.

"Teach me, Lola."

"With an audience?"

"All I see is you."

And she got it. Got how he felt, how she consumed him because her world was just as focused.

"We need a prenup," Ogilvie said. "Airtight, this can't be the last—"

"Detroit," Ballard said randomly, probably to avert disaster. "Get them on the phone, make your priorities clear."

Time for her to chime in. "You're opening a Crimson in Detroit now too?"

"We have a manufacturing plant up there," Zairn said.

She hadn't known that. Getting up to speed would take some time. "Who is 'we'? Rouge?"

"Us," he said, smiling at her. "What's mine is yours."

"Cool," she said and sniffed. "I always wanted a manufacturing plant."

"Would you like me to put in the call?" Tibbs asked.

From Rome? How would he connect them?

"No, I have the other call first. Family takes priority."

Roxie exaggerated her scan of the room. "Your family are all here. Unless you mean Knox?"

"I need to return a call from Blayne."

"Blayne?" she asked, scrunching her face before gasping. "Oh my God, you do not mean my sister's loser boyfriend!"

"We don't get to pick 'em," he said. "Maybe your

sister says the same about yours."

"You are not a loser mooching off my mom. I'll kill him. How did he get your number?"

"I suppose from your sister."

"She doesn't have…" Leaping up to whirl around, she pointed at the TV. "Astrid. My sister called you. After Sydney, you were in touch with each other."

The young woman nodded. Roxie screeched.

"It's okay," Zairn said. "I'll return the call and—"

"No! No. Absolutely not! You are not allowed to call him." She turned her attention back to the TV. "Astrid, Tibbs, burn his number." About-facing, she marched in the direction of the bedroom. "I'll take care of this myself."

FOUR

"BLAYNE'S JUST… I can't believe he would do that!"

"Call up your boyfriend?" Toria asked from Roxie's phone propped on the closet vanity. "Yes, you can. He's a total leech."

"A letch?" Jane asked, reappearing on the screen.

"A leech," Toria said, correcting the mistake. "He takes and takes. He's practically moved in with her parents."

"Did Zairn go crazy?"

"Did…? No!" Roxie said, slipping on her ruby again. Even just taking it off to shower seemed too long. She flashed it at the phone camera. "My ruby's too big to disappear down a shower drain… right?"

"Yeah, yeah, we get it," Toria said, dropping back in the couch. "You're Miss Money Bags now."

"I'll let you borrow it," she said, then scrunched her nose and shook her head. "No, I won't… but we'll get you rubies for your birthday, how about that?"

Toria smiled while Jane was more discerning. "What about the Queens? Are they still allowed to be a thing?"

The Queens had lost their status during the Gambatto debacle. Whether or not they'd been reinstated… she'd never asked.

"I'm not going to change things," Roxie said. "We talked about this. Crimson is still Zairn's, he's still in charge."

"Yeah, but you could revoke their status, if you wanted."

She shrugged. "Guess it depended what mood Ballard was in when I asked… It's in my interest for Queens to remain a thing. Crimson has to stay cool, coveted… what will my children inherit otherwise?"

"Have you talked about the wedding?" Jane said, barely containing her excitement. "Please tell me you have a date… have you decided on a location?"

"Give her a break," Toria said. "If Zairn Lomond was your fiancé, how much time would you want to spend talking? Seriously? I thought we wouldn't see her for days… that we'd have to intervene to stop her parents reporting her missing."

Her friend was only half kidding. If she wanted to lock herself in the suite with Zairn, she'd find a way to persuade him.

"We talked a little about it last night," she said, inspiring Jane to squee some. "Didn't come to any final decisions."

"The guest list will be epic," Toria said, threading her fingers through Jane's. "Good thing we're both single. We better keep it that way. Zairn knows a bunch of rich, famous people."

"He does," Roxie said. "I don't know, we'll talk about that at the club tonight."

"I thought you wanted to go to the CollCom studio today?"

"Yeah, we have to do more editing stuff. I'm excited! You guys will be able to see more of the tour!"

"And you can tell us when and where you screwed around the world."

That was actually a sad, sort of pathetic list given everywhere they'd traveled on the tour. Rome was their first night together… Apart from that, had they done it anywhere outside the US? Barcelona? No. London? No. They'd have to remedy that… it could be added to the list after everything else.

"The wedding is important," Jane said. "Really important… I can go grab some magazines—"

"Not today," Roxie said.

Talking to Jane about the planning thing first was essential. Before her friend got any ideas about going overboard. Yes, it would mean a lot to her, but it also had to be their day… Though, in truth, there was a grateful selfish part of her that she wouldn't have to deal with all that hullabaloo.

"Don't you want to get started sooner rather than later?" Jane asked with complete conviction. "Some places are reserved years and years in advance. You want to get on it fast, trust me."

"We will," Roxie said, raking a finger through her little box of earrings to pick one out. When she held it up to her ear to check her reflection, Zairn appeared in the closet door further along the wall, typing something into his phone. "Do you think it's okay for a billionaire's fiancée to wear CZs?"

Her girls inhaled to respond, but her man's muttered response came first. "Give them to Tibbs, he'll have diamonds put in."

"Into plated silver? This is costume jewelry, honey, from the discount aisle."

He slipped his phone in his pocket. "Okay, so give them to Tibbs and he'll have custom replicas made, top quality gems set in platinum."

She huffed. "Wow, what a snob. Not everything is about money, you know."

Wearing a half smile, he came to press a kiss to her hair, then carried on to his own side of the closet.

"It's so weird," Jane whispered.

Even Toria leaned in and they were in the same room.

Roxie bent closer to her phone. "What are you talking about?"

"Zairn Lomond," Jane whispered, cupping a hand around her mouth. "Right there."

"I know," Roxie declared, standing upright. "I got my breakfast from his balls this morning."

Jane gasped while Toria laughed. She'd moved on to a different pair of earrings but did notice him turn in her periphery.

"Where was I for that?" he asked, wandering her way. "Maybe next time you're ordering off menu, page me first."

"Nobody pages anyone anymore," she said, bumping her butt on him when he reached her.

That encouraged him to take her hips and pull her back against him. "You don't need earrings in bed," he mumbled in her hair.

She put in an earring. "I'm not going to bed, I'm going out." He turned her to press her up against the vanity as she put in the second earring, a feral smile on his face. "You chose to get out of bed and leave me there. Naked. Hot… Wet for you."

"You're always wet for me, baby."

Her own smile was difficult to keep at bay, especially when he ducked to kiss her.

"Uh, you know we're still here?" Jane asked.

"Shhh!" Toria objected. "We were about to get a live action show."

"I'll get you downstairs in ten minutes," Roxie said, wriggling around to face the mirror and retrieve her phone. "That gives him eight minutes of cuddle time."

She hung up and he whirled her around to pick her up and set her on the vanity. "Eight minutes of cuddle time?"

Shrugging, she pushed out her chest. "They're jealous enough already. A totally hunky, super rich, incredibly besotted international playboy just proposed to me."

"Oh yeah?" he asked, sweeping her hair from her shoulder to kiss her neck. "What was your answer?"

Slipping off her shoes, she locked her legs around him. "That my boyfriend isn't in to sharing."

"Good answer."

"I have to go," she said when he kissed her again. "And Blayne won't call you again. Ever. You should change your number."

"To hide from your family?"

"And to cut off all the 'hos from your past. You're a

one woman guy now, Casanova."

"Thought you liked me having a girl in every port."

"I do." She grinned, planting her hands on his cheeks to pull his attention to her eyes. "And I can be in every one with just a little notice."

"In everyone? Am I in this monogamous relationship by myself?"

"Sure. What if John D. Rockerduck or Flintheart Glomgold become available?" He frowned. "Too obscure? See, I knew you didn't watch cartoons."

"I watch you," he murmured in her ear, trailing his lips down the side of her neck. "My girl."

"Yours," she said, her head sinking to the side. "Forever and always."

He groaned. "And I didn't think you could get any sexier."

"Baby," she said, seeking his belt. "You know we're in a closet again."

Leaning back, he sought her gaze. "You just lie in wait for me, don't you?"

Her fiancé was hilarious. "And no one can prove otherwise…" She checked her invisible watch. "You're cutting into our cuddle time."

"Screw cuddling," he said, driving his hands under her ass to pick her up and lay her on the floor.

Yep, that sounded good to her. Less cuddling meant more together time.

FIVE

DRESSING UP WAS always fun. Even if she had done it more since Zairn came into her life, the experience was still enjoyable… and the dresses sure had gotten more expensive.

With her ruby on her hand, she didn't need other accessories. Maybe if she got little studs to match. Nothing fancy, just something simple to contrast her dark hair. Thank God she looked good in red, it was becoming her signature color.

A purse was pointless too. Wasn't like her phone would last the night… Where was her phone anyway? Wherever it was, it wouldn't be charged. Drinks were free, her ruby was her security pass, and she didn't need a key for the suite… did she? After Talk at Sunset, her face probably worked just as well.

After glossing her lips, she stuck the tube in her cleavage and nodded at her reflection. Her girls were in their room downstairs getting ready. They'd gotten a lot done in the editing suite, though the documentary was shaping up to be like twenty hours long.

Hatfield would handle it… that was his job, right?

After eating dinner in her roommates' suite, they'd turned on the music and had a few drinks. Crimson was inevitable. They wanted to celebrate in their own typical fashion.

For a second, she considered leaving a note for Zairn. Without her phone, she couldn't text him. Hmm. He'd check the club if he was looking for her, wouldn't he? It wasn't like he had to worry about her safety.

She hadn't seen him all day and didn't want to be one of those sad sap types who had to be with their partner every minute. But God, did she miss him. Crazy! They'd seen each other a few hours ago and had spent longer apart in the past. Still, it was what it was.

Turned out she didn't have to miss him for much longer. When heading out, she discovered him sitting at the bar in their suite, Knox on the other side.

Zairn turned toward her, opening an arm. "Where have you been?"

Tipping her head back, she pushed her hair from her shoulders. "Downstairs for dinner, then up here getting ready." She took his outstretched hand to step in closer, wrapping his arm around her waist. "Did you miss me?"

"I did," he said, accepting her quick kiss.

"Wow," she said, smiling. "I'm surprised you said that in front of your buddy."

"His buddy knows he's sunk," Knox said, tossing back a shot of something. "You look good."

"Thanks," she said, narrowing her eyes on him. "Do I want to know what's going on with you?"

Her fiancé was the one to answer. "No," he said and kissed her cheek before nuzzling her hair aside. "I'll tell you later."

And he would if she asked. Looking him in the eye again, she planted one short, hard kiss on his lips then extricated herself.

"Where are you going?" Zairn asked. "You want a drink?"

"I had one downstairs. I'm going to meet my girls."

"Why?"

"We're going to a club."

"Anywhere I know?" he asked as she swerved around him.

"No," she said, turning to walk backwards, maintaining her momentum. "It's super hip and cool, not your kind of place… it's exclusive clientele only. You wouldn't get in." Enjoying her own joke, she turned away to continue a couple of steps before stopping. Spinning to face him again, she blinked while he raised his brows in question. "Will I get in?"

Immediately, he frowned. "I thought you were kidding around."

"I was."

"If you're not going to Crimson, where you going?"

"I am going to Crimson."

Another frown. "And you think you won't get in? You've seen the news, right? You know you're screwing the owner? Said so right there on TV."

"I don't believe in TV, only the internet," she said, sashaying toward him. "I haven't had the best luck with Crimson LA. First time, I got arrested. Second, I was dumped."

Zairn smiled. "Your ruby gets you in anywhere. And your security detail is waiting downstairs with your driver."

"My security detail. Always with the security detail." She laid her hands on his shirt. "Will you come make out with me later?"

"You could stay and have sex instead of going out."

Her arching side nod was deliberately theatrical. "That Collier guy's watching," she whispered from the corner of her mouth.

"I'm sure he'll get the hint when I strip you naked."

She glanced at her dress. "You know this thing is basically hanging by a thread." The spaghetti halter wouldn't take long to shed. Gripping his shirt, she groaned. "I want to replace the bad memory with a good one. And we stayed in last night. You have your whole life to screw me raw."

Knox laughed. "Wow, and they say romance is dead? Obviously, they haven't heard your brand of poetry, RK."

"Where's your fiancée, Knox?" she asked, knowing he didn't have one. "I'm marrying this guy, which means I'll be around when you find her… I can make it easy on you or difficult."

"Who fixed you two up again?" Fair point, but it wasn't under his own initiative. "We're coming to the club later anyway."

Her attention snapped to Zairn. "So why argue with me? What if I'd said yes to sex? I'd be naked, waiting for cock, left hanging… I'd have to call the concierge to send up an erect bellhop or something. You want some nineteen-year-old, minimum wage grunt doing your duties? Does that sound fair, Casanova?"

Zairn straightened his arm to free his watch from his cuff to read it. "I have a few minutes to squeeze you in."

"Laugh it up," she said. "Tomorrow's headline will read, 'billionaire business mogul and media magnate buddy, refused entry to exclusive club.'"

Her fiancé smiled while his friend's head tilted. "Not one for brevity?"

"That's not my style, Collier," she said. "Not my style at all."

Zairn caught her hand to pull her back to him. "Come here."

"Baby," she whimpered. "If you kiss me like I want you to kiss me, I'll be late for my girls again… you know, like I was earlier? Remember? You? Me? Closet?"

"I just want to give you something."

She glanced at Knox again. "You want to avert your eyes? You know, be polite? I'm his fiancée, not one of his spring break coeds… New rules, no witnesses to sex." Zairn put something in her hand. Her phone. "Huh… how did you do that?"

"It's charged. Keep it close."

"Okay," she said, thinking a purse was now required. Jane would have one. Jane always had a purse.

After another quick kiss, he let her back away.

"You going to be good?" he asked.

She shrugged. "Probably not."

A glimpse of his smile joined her as she began to turn away.

"Hey," he said and she turned back. "Catch."

He tossed something across the room, and it was an absolute wonder that she caught it. A box… A jewelry box. Popping it open, the diamond and ruby earrings inside were gorgeous. Simple. Perfect. One drop diamond stud hooked to a teardrop ruby. How had he done that? It wasn't like her to get emotional, so the heat in her eyes took her by surprise.

Maybe it was the way she chewed her lip, or maybe he just saw it in her eyes, but his smile faded when she looked up at him.

"What's wrong?"

Shaking her head, she was aware tears might win if she spoke. "Nothing."

He stood up.

Knox took another shot. "Uh oh, you've broken her."

"Lola…" Zairn said, crossing to her. "What is it?"

"You know I don't need sparkly things, right? That I don't love you for sparkly things?"

"If they piss you off, we'll get rid of them," he said, closing the box, trying to take it from her hand.

She clung to it, pulling it to her chest. "No, I love them. I want them, I… They're perfect."

Even better than the earrings she'd envisioned.

With her hands occupied, she could only loop her arms around his neck, but managed to pull him down for a kiss. Damnit. Now sex was unavoidable. Not for the gems, for his innate knowing of her… Her girls would understand.

SIX

THE STAR TREATMENT she'd received before was nothing to what she got now that she was engaged to the owner.

Not only was her every whim catered to, but her authority was relied upon. Staff came to ask questions of what was allowed and got her go ahead when patrons made requests. The frequency of visits became so regular that Toria began to field them, telling people to back off. Was it the novelty of the relationship or did Zairn deal with that kind of pestering every day?

The private pods of the LA club were a godsend. To get away from those crowding her, she and her girls headed into the central one, Zairn's favorite… and also the place he'd dumped her. Hmm, maybe they should do a remodel.

They'd just gotten new drinks and she used the app on her phone to adjust the pod's music. Not a bad gig.

"You're different," Toria said.

Both of her friends were smiling at her.

"Me?" Roxie asked, touching the surface of her drink. "Why am I different?"

"You're in lurve," Toria exaggerated the tease.

"Don't make fun of her," Jane said in typical swoon

style. "It's sweet… You're so lucky."

"I know," Roxie said. "Another couple of weeks and he'll put me on his bank account for sure."

Toria switched focus to Jane. "So when are you quitting your job?"

"Quitting?" Jane asked. "I can't quit my job."

"We told Rox if she moved to New York, we'd move with her, right?"

"I know, but—"

"Uh, uh, no but. We said so."

"Before that," Roxie said, slipping off her shoes. "We need to make plans."

"For?" Toria asked through narrowed eyes. "Moving to New York."

It amazed her that Toria wasn't facing the obvious. "We both know Jane will work her notice. Even if I tell her Zairn will make a call, she'll still insist on doing it."

Toria nodded along despite Jane's squeaks of affronted protest. Well, as affronted as Jane could ever be. Their friend didn't like to make waves… or let anyone down.

"I am right here," Jane said, attracting their attention.

"Am I wrong?" Roxie asked, tucking her feet up beside her. "You want Z to make a call?"

Her friend's shoulders dropped, she held her breath for a second, then exhaled. "No."

"Okay."

Except Jane wasn't done. "I can't quit my job. What if I don't get another job? I could ask for a transfer."

"You could," Roxie said, nodding along, thinking Zairn could make a call about that too.

"Who are you kidding?" Toria asked. "We're going to live with Roxie. In Zairn's place. In New York. He covers the bills, you don't even need a job. We'll mooch off Roxie, like Blayne does her mom… You'll repay him in sex, won't you, honey?"

"No way!" Roxie teased. "He gets the privilege of being Mr Roxie Kyst, *he* pays *me* in sex."

Though they'd had so much of it in the last twenty-four hours, she'd guess they were paying each other… or trying to save the earth with it.

"Zairn's people live at Crimson," Jane said. "He has a whole floor of apartments for employees."

Hmm, she didn't know that. "He does?"

"Oh, God, yes he does!" Toria burst in. "My God, we can live there… Wait, did we just talk ourselves out of living with Zairn?"

"Sean Ballard lives there," Jane said like Toria hadn't spoken. "Astrid. Zairn's assistant. Ogilvie too."

That put a smile on her face. "You mean I can rush down to freak out Ogilvie any time I want?"

"They don't pay rent. It's part of their salary."

"Yeah, 'cause they're hardly ever there. Who would pay for an apartment full time when they spend their lives traveling the globe," Roxie said. "If there are empty apartments, I'll talk to Zairn. You won't be on the street, if you have to live with us, you can."

"Have to?"

"Yeah, well, we'll have a lot of sex whenever we're home."

Home. Zairn's apartment. New York. Not so long ago, she'd been resistant to uniting their lives. Thank God she got her head out her ass in time. Imagine it had taken seeing him with someone else to give her the kick she needed.

A chill went through her.

Toria raised a hand. "I don't mind if he walks around naked."

"They'll want to be alone. Newly affianced. Almost married… then you'll be newlywed thinking about kids."

"Funny you should bring that up," Roxie said, going in easy.

Jane shrieked. "Oh my God! You're already pregnant?" She lunged over to take Roxie's glass. "You shouldn't be drinking that."

While Jane glanced around looking for a way to get rid of it, Toria reached over from behind and snagged the glass to down the contents.

"Oh, great, thanks," Roxie said, laying a pointed look on Jane. "No, I am not pregnant. I meant bringing up the wedding."

"When have you had a chance to talk about it? We were together all day."

"I told you we talked a little bit last night, we decided we need a wedding planner."

"Good idea! So long as it's a good one. Someone who listens and doesn't just gouge you for a check."

"Glad you think so," Roxie said, glancing at the curious Toria, Jane was her oblivious self. "So after you've worked your notice… you'll work for us?"

Immediately, Toria whooped and leaped from her armchair to bounce onto the couch to hug the dumbfounded Jane from behind. "Did you hear that, honey? You get to plan Roxie's wedding… it'll be like a dry run for yours… You better bag a billionaire, Jane, babe. You'll get an appetite for it, and it suits you…" Toria lifted her head. "Z will hook her up, right?"

"Sure!"

"How much notice do you have to give?" Toria asked. "We can't send her back to Chicago alone."

Roxie shrugged. "I don't know if I'll be joining the Retrospective or if I have to stay in LA for more edits. I think Hatfield is coming back into town for a while. Though maybe he won't if he has both Z and I on the tour… He's probably pissed he missed out on the big scoop."

Was their relationship a scoop? If Zairn's people suspected something was going on between them, the documentary director couldn't have missed it.

"The editing was fun," Toria said. "I can deal with the Hatfield guy if he comes back. You go home with Jane and pack up the apartment or, even better, go with Zairn."

That would be a dream. And give her a chance to check a few foreign countries off her sexual bucket list.

"I'll talk to him," Roxie said. "Jane, would you be okay back home yourself? It shouldn't just fall to her to pack our crap too."

"I can help," Toria said, going back to her chair, and her drink. "When the editing stuff is done. We'll have like a month, right?"

"You don't think I should get a transfer to the New York office?"

"How are you going to plan their wedding and hold down a full-time job?"

"We don't want you to do anything you don't want to," Roxie said. "Work if you want to work, we'd never tell you not to… Not like there's any hurry for the wedding."

"No!" Jane exclaimed, bouncing closer. "There's hurry. You can't be one of those couples who are just engaged forever. No way."

The door opened and a server came in with a tray of drinks. Good, she needed one. Didn't take long to notice there were more than just three glasses. Apparently, they were due guests.

A moment after the server left, the door opened again. Zairn strolled in with Knox.

"Ladies," her guy said in greeting.

"We were just talking about the wedding," Roxie said when he sat at her side and laid an arm across her lap.

"Oh, yeah?" he asked and looked to Jane. "Will you help us out?"

Her friend stayed still, like maybe she could turn invisible.

Roxie leaned closer. "Maybe best not to look directly at her, baby."

"You have to get over your starstruck thing, Jane," Toria said. "You'll have to be calling him up about measurements and cake design and what else do rich people have? Oh! You should get a horse and carriage!"

The rise of Zairn's brows was hilarious. "Don't worry, Casanova, at the end of the day, you'll have the girl… forever."

Even though she deliberately tried to make that sound daunting, he just smiled and kissed her.

"We have to make decisions," Toria said. "Obviously, Jane and I will be bridesmaids."

"And Astrid."

"Astrid, absolutely, what about your sister?"

After that morning… "I don't know if I even want

my family there."

She'd get over it… maybe.

"Who's your best man going to be?" Toria asked and pointed at Knox in the opposite armchair. "Knox?"

Roxie stroked Zairn's leg. "Ballard would be honored too."

"Yeah," Knox said, smirking. "You'll have trouble narrowing it down. Could be anyone in our secret posse."

"Reid stood up for Kintyre."

"So we have to trade off?" Knox asked. "'Cause Reid asked Rourke. It's not tit for tat."

"You'll ask Camden," Zairn said.

"Only to drag him back kicking and screaming," Knox said, amused. "That mean I'm out the running? If it's not me, it's Dyce, Gauge, or Peake? Go with the last and maybe he'll sell to you."

Zairn laughed. "Just to screw the guys over?"

Knox raised his hands from the arms of the chair. "All's fair in love and business, right? Isn't that the motto?"

Roxie couldn't believe it, she was actually agog. Too bad neither of the men noticed. She poked Zairn's chest repeatedly until he drew his attention to her.

"Uh, hello?" she said, blinking at him.

He stroked her cheek. "Hey."

"No, not hey," she said, pushing his hand away. "I'm your fiancée!"

"Right," he said, question in his eyes. "You want everyone to clear out so we can—"

"No! What is this secret posse? You have a secret posse? Why don't I know you have a secret posse?" She gestured at the women. "You know all about my posse! I should know about yours!"

"It's not a secret."

"Sure it is," Knox said, apparently relishing dropping his friend in the shit. "We don't advertise our associations."

"Not advertising them and keeping them secret are two different things."

"If you want to split hairs with the missus."

While Zairn looked from his friend to her, he'd only

read agreement on her face. Yeah, Knox was stirring things up for fun, but his point was valid.

"It's not a secret," he said, trying to take her hand. "Lola, come on, if it was a secret, why would I have brought it up?"

"You didn't. Toria asked the question and Knox told the truth. Maybe you should be more like Mr. Collier."

"Cool," Knox said. "Respect."

"So…" Roxie said, tilting her head. "What's your secret posse?"

Zairn knew everyone. Many people. And had connections all over the world. It wasn't that she minded him knowing people, she just didn't like being out of the loop.

"Baby, I don't…" He must have read her insistence and exhaled. "It's no secret. Just some guys I went to school with. We keep in touch. Help each other out. We're not on the phone every day of the week."

"Unless there's a crisis," Knox interjected.

"Well, yeah."

"Or big news."

Okay the flash of Zairn's glare shot around to his grinning friend.

"I want to meet them," she said, stroking Zairn's cheek to get his attention back. "I want to be in your secret posse."

"You're as unsecret as my posse gets," he said. "You'll meet them. They're eager to meet you."

"Where are they?"

"All over, Lola. They have their own shit going on."

"More important than me."

He bowed closer. "They're getting used to my crisis event."

She smiled and looped her arm around his. "Are they involved?"

"Buyer's remorse?" Zairn asked, touching her ruby.

Maintaining eye contact, she tightened her embrace. "I have single friends, baby… And I have to know which of your friends might lead you astray."

"Knox," Zairn said, pointing. "If you want me to cut

him out, I'll do it. Without hesitation."

"That's how much you love me?" she asked, restraining a laugh.

"That's right," he said, smirking. "Just for you, gorgeous."

The truth was somewhere closer to winding up his friend after he stirred the pot, but the tease was sweet and exactly what she expected from her guy.

SEVEN

THE BED MOVED. Or she did. No, Zairn wasn't under her head anymore. Hmm. Her heat was gone.

"Trust Z to be the one with a woman in his bed," a male said.

A male she didn't recognize.

"Don't wake her. Trust me."

Okay, that voice she did recognize. Knox. Was he there? They didn't sound like in the room voices. If she turned over to check, they'd change their behaviors. She wanted to know who these people were in their natural state.

"She's not a woman," Z said. "She's my fiancée."

"Yeah, I heard LA could change a man."

Laughter. How many men? More than three.

Z followed with his own humorless laugh. "I meant she's my fiancée, she's trusted. Forget about her, tell us what's going on."

"You need an update," another different unknown male said.

"You dropping out?"

"No, worse," a third guy. "He's engaged."

"What?" Knox asked, clearly surprised. "This from the guy who said never again?"

"Kintyre and Peake aren't here," Zairn said. "They're not just busy, this is about Gramercy."

"Right. The engagement is not real. It's something we need to get the deal through."

"Past Madelyn, you mean," Knox said. "Do you trust her? Your fiancée?"

"Do we know her?" Zairn asked.

"No, she works at RCI."

"An employee? Shit, Reid."

All these males… this was his secret posse. Maybe she should've slept over with him more often.

"How'd you pick her?"

"Not important. You'll get the news in a couple of hours."

"And everything's no comment."

"Yeah, no shit," Zairn said. "Have you prepped her?"

"For what?"

"The storm ahead. She doesn't only have to fight off your stalker of an ex, she's moving into dating the CEO territory."

"And you'll be moving her in," Knox said. "Does she know that?"

"Not yet."

"It's a lot to handle. You better be sure she's strong enough for it."

"She hot?"

"And this is why we don't invite you to shit, Gauge."

"It matters. It has to look real. And, apparently, being a fiancée doesn't automatically mean trust. Your engagement real, Z? Or is she a front for something too?"

Laughter. Why was that funny?

"If you haven't seen my relationship with the Empress play out on screens around the world, you've been living under a rock. It's real."

"That's nothing to seeing the two of you together," Knox said. "And no one else saw her determination when she showed up in my office. It's real. Roxie is smitten."

"Who wouldn't be?" Zairn asked.

Staying quiet and still had never been so difficult.

"Can't wait to meet her in person."

"Yeah, the feeling's mutual. We'll figure something out. Right now, the concern is your fake fiancée. Roxie can handle anything, would handle anything, but she has the relationship to back it up. You prepared to support this stranger through what's about to happen? I don't know her, but unless she's made of steel, she will need someone to talk to, someone to reassure her."

"Z is right." Who was that? "She needs someone to hold her hand."

Married to the CEO. Employee? Probably a lower tax bracket. The poor woman had no idea what lay ahead. And there was an ex in the mix? A stalker ex? Yowsa!

"I'll go," she said, stretching as she rolled to her back. "Babe?"

"Guess she's not as sleeping as you thought."

The TV was out of its hidey-hole at the end of the bed and high enough that Zairn was standing to the side with it at his eye level. Tilted toward him, she could only see it from an angle.

"Whoever this woman is, she doesn't have a clue what she's about to live through," she said, sitting up in a stretch, just catching the sheet before it fell from her chest. Maybe naked wasn't the best way to meet Zairn's friends. "And there's no prize at the end for her."

"Like fifty grand?" Knox asked, smirking.

Roxie frowned at her fiancé. "That's right. You stiffed me for fifty grand."

"I'm marrying you in lieu of that," he said, mischief glittering from him. He better be careful. She was naked in bed. If he turned her on, she'd stop caring about the audience. "I'll be stiffing you the rest of your life."

"And if I die first?" she said, gesturing at the screen. "I have witnesses, I expect you to mourn forever. Your cock will be in retirement."

"Nah, by then I'll be at the perfect age to marry a nineteen-year-old Playboy bunny who'll pressure me into changing my will, screwing over our kids."

"Man's living the dream," one of the on-screen guys

said.

"And you wonder why Reid swore off it?" another said.

Knox shook his head. "Swearing off marriage, I understand. Camden's life choice on the other hand…"

Some of the guys on screen laughed, others were more subdued. Sheesh, buy a sense of humor. Though, she was intrigued, what life choice did this Camden make?

"He's always been the black sheep," one of the guys on-screen said.

"Let's call it what it is, he's weird. Flat out strange. A freak. Always was. Who walks away from their trust fund? Did you ever get a psych profile?"

Black sheep. That guy was familiar. In the darkness with the TV brightness low, it wasn't immediately obvious. When it struck her, she clung tighter to the sheet and bounced closer to Zairn, her eyes locked on the screen.

"You're Zane Dyce."

He smiled. "Nice to meet you."

Zairn pointed at the screen with the remote. "Left to right, Matteo Reid, Xavien Rourke, Zane Dyce. Xander Gauge is underneath, Knox you know."

"Hey, Rox," Knox said. "Sure you want to leave your fiancé so soon after your engagement?"

Reid. That was the name used of the affianced guy. First box.

"Where is Reid?"

"Manhattan."

"Oh, that's fine," she said, turning a broad smile to her fiancé. "We live in New York. Guy doesn't even have to give me a bed."

"We have the Retrospective and I know you were enjoying—"

"You can do the Retrospective," she said, her grip increasing. "Toria will stay here for the edits, I can work on it from Manhattan with her. It'll only be a week or two. Let's face it, we'll have to get used to being apart sometimes." He didn't appear convinced, her head dropped to the side. "You know I can handle anything."

"If you're happy, I'm happy."

"This is important to your friend," Roxie said, then admitted another truth. "If this woman is unprepared, the scam will fall apart before it begins and then what happens? Your friend is humiliated and whatever this is really about is ruined."

"I'll regret saying this in front of her..." Knox started, "but there's no one else I'd trust to do it. Any of the rest of us would be too high profile."

"Yeah, we'd grab headlines of our own."

"And she'll relate to a woman easier than a guy."

Her brows rose. "Are you all reaching the conclusion I got to five minutes ago?"

From the various stunned expressions on the screen, she'd guess these men weren't used to being sassed. Poor guys. Didn't know what life was.

Knox laughed. "Your introduction to Roxanna Kyst, men. Baptism by fire."

"Smitten?" she asked him.

"I backed you up... twice."

With the string pulling for Talk at Sunset and just now with her idea.

"Okay," she conceded. "Just don't go telling other people. His head is big enough already."

"You want Roxie or not?" Zairn asked. "Gotta admit, I'm reluctant to send her over there."

"'Cause you're smitten?" she asked, teasing him.

"That," he said, accepting the accusation. "And because I actually like these guys. I'm not sure inflicting you on them would be fair."

"They didn't get to where they were by being scared of tough talk."

"It's less the tough talk and more the smart mouth that concerns me," he said, sitting on the bed next to her. "I'll send you if you promise to reserve the sass for me."

Leaning closer, she watched his mouth. "What do I get in return?"

His smirk lingered on her. "I'll put her on a plane tomorrow, Reid," he said and raised the remote to blank the screen.

As it descended into the base of the bed again, he tossed the remote away and crawled over her as she lay on her back.

"Any more than two weeks and I'm coming to find you."

"That'll give me enough time to sell everything of value in your apartment… and change a few things around the Crimson flagship venue."

"Whatever makes you happy, Lola," he said and kissed her.

Running her fingers into his hair, she eased from their kiss. "I want to help out your friend… to be in your secret posse."

"You are the be all and end all, baby. Without you, there's nothing else."

"Charmer," she said, aware he was teasing. "Do you mind me staying in your place in New York? If it's a problem—"

"Our place," he said. "You have full access. I'll speak to Reid tomorrow, make sure you're approved at his too. Zane designed all the systems, so we have access to each other's—"

"When I'm on the plane tomorrow, you'll regret talking so much tonight."

Another smile. "Damnit, I love you, Lola."

"I love you too, Casanova."

As he kissed her again, she closed her eyes tighter, determined to memorize every second of being beneath him. They were strong. Secure. Together. That didn't mean she wouldn't miss him.

Read more from the Roxiverse in
Nothing to Declare...

Thank you for reading this tale!
If you can, please take the time to review.

~

Ask your local library for more Scarlett Finn
novels!

~

For all things Scarlett Finn
check out:

www.scarlettfinn.com

Next in the

Roxiverse: